NOWHERE IN SIGHT!

Underfoot, the tabby cat, the Irish setter, the parrot, and the snake were still meowing and barking and squawking and slithering, when the door to the vet's office suddenly swung open and Officer Roseberg stepped inside.

"What's going on in here?" she cried. She shut the door behind her quickly—but just before it closed, Underfoot darted outside.

"Underfoot! Oh, no! Underfoot!" Jimmy yelped. He hurtled over the animals, past Officer Roseberg, and out into the street.

Jimmy looked all around but Underfoot was nowhere in sight! Where had he gone?

THE MANY LIVES OF
UNDERFOOT
THE
CAT

Trouble
AND
More Trouble

By Jack Maguire
Illustrated by Sandy Kossin
Produced by The Philip Lief Group

A
MINSTREL®
BOOK

PUBLISHED BY POCKET BOOKS

New York   London   Toronto   Sydney   Tokyo   Singapore

A MINSTREL PAPERBACK *ORIGINAL*

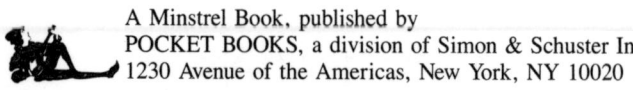A Minstrel Book, published by
POCKET BOOKS, a division of Simon & Schuster Inc.
1230 Avenue of the Americas, New York, NY 10020

ISBN: 0-671-64042-9

First Minstrel Books Printing November 1990

10   9   8   7   6   5   4   3   2   1

A MINSTREL BOOK and colophon are registered trademarks
of Simon & Schuster Inc.

Printed in the U.S.A.

To Sam, Rocky, Maggie, Rex, Sophie, Starbuck, Overton, Casey, and Tracy—my excellent guides through the animal kingdom

TROUBLE

O N E

══ THE VANISHING ACT ══

Jimmy Clark leaned out the front window of his new apartment on the fifth floor of 237 Washington Street. Behind him, painters were busy turning the dirty gray walls of the dining room into bright blue walls. In front of him lay the roofs and treetops of his new neighborhood. The view was okay, Jimmy thought, but somehow it made him feel lonely. "Who lives in all these places?" he wondered. "What will fourth grade be like here?"

Jimmy had just spotted the three-story school he would go to in September, when he heard his mother yelling from the front door.

"James Finnington Clark!" she cried.

Jimmy's mother hardly ever called him by his

full name. When she did, watch out! Jimmy raced to her side, wondering what was wrong.

"What on earth are these?" exclaimed Mrs. Clark, pointing to the floor.

Jimmy gasped. Running along the floor from the paint-spattered sheet in the dining room to the front door were neat little blue paw prints!

"Wow, Mom. I swear, I don't know what they are!" Jimmy answered at last. He dropped to the floor and touched one of the prints. "Almost dry," he announced. He studied the tracks. "They're way too big to be rat prints!"

"Yes, that's true, thank goodness," replied his mother. "And they're way too small to be tiger prints." Mrs. Clark smiled. "It looks as if we have a mystery on our hands, but I don't have time to worry about it now."

Mrs. Clark was a photographer. She had spent all morning in her darkroom working on a special feature for the Sunday newspaper—pictures of oddly shaped fruits and vegetables.

"Would you please try to clean up the paint for me, Jimmy?" she asked. "I've got to get back to my Statue of Liberty potato."

"Sure, Mom," Jimmy said, trying not to laugh. But he did not head for the cleaning rags right away. He wanted to investigate the prints first.

Jimmy opened the front door and followed the blue marks down the fifth floor corridor. They led Jimmy past the stairway and around the corner, growing fainter with every step. At last they disappeared in front of the elevator.

"Awesome!" Jimmy whispered to himself. "Just like a ghost!" He lay down on his stomach so he could look at the prints more closely.

Suddenly the elevator door opened. A large woman backed out, pulling a small cart piled high with groceries. Jimmy didn't recognize the woman until she turned around. She was Mrs. Bruno, who lived in apartment 5B, next door to Jimmy and his family in 5A. She taught music at Claremont Elementary, the school Jimmy had seen out the window a few minutes earlier.

"Good afternoon, Jimmy Clark," Mrs. Bruno said. "Why are you lying on the floor?"

"Hello, Mrs. Bruno," Jimmy said, scrambling to his feet. "I was checking out these paw prints.

Something mysterious got into our apartment, stepped in our paint, and then came out here in the hallway and vanished!"

"Aha!" Mrs. Bruno responded as she kneeled to examine the tracks herself. "It must have been that Underfoot monster."

Jimmy's eyes widened with curiosity. "Underfoot?" he repeated.

"That's what everyone here calls him," Mrs. Bruno replied. Jimmy tagged along behind her as she pulled her cart toward the other end of the building. "He's a cat—a very independent, secretive, mischief-making cat. He sneaks all over the building, popping in and out of places, poking his nose into everyone's business, and always causing trouble!"

"Wow!" Jimmy exclaimed. "How long has this been going on?"

"As I recall, Underfoot first showed up a few weeks ago," Mrs. Bruno said. "Right after school let out in June. I'm surprised you haven't run into him before. I'm sure he knows every nook and cranny of your apartment by now!"

"Where did Underfoot come from?" Jimmy

asked, growing excited. "Does he belong to anyone?"

"I don't know where he came from," Mrs. Bruno replied. "He certainly doesn't belong to anyone—nobody can catch him! And if someone did catch him, well, think of the trouble Underfoot would be!"

"Underfoot must be pretty smart," Jimmy said. He was impressed. He didn't care if Mrs. Bruno thought Underfoot was trouble.

"Oh, he's a sly one, all right," declared Mrs. Bruno. "He got into the flower box in my living room window one rainy afternoon and tracked dark brown mud all over my new white carpet!"

"Have you ever seen Underfoot?" Jimmy asked. "What does he look like?"

"Like a little bandit!" Mrs. Bruno exclaimed, as she opened her front door. "Let me know if you ever catch him. I'd like to shake the nine lives right out of him!"

That night, Jimmy couldn't fall asleep. The smell of fresh paint and the excitement of the day made him restless. His eyes darted around his room, but there was nothing much to see. The walls were still bare, waiting to be painted. And most of his toys and clothes were still packed in boxes. Finally, he just stared at the full moon shining through the fire escape outside his window.

"Underfoot, Underfoot, Underfoot," Jimmy said dreamily, thinking of the bandit cat.

All at once a masked figure was staring back at Jimmy from the other side of the window. Jimmy was wide awake. His heart seemed to stop for a moment, until he realized who the figure was.

It was Underfoot!

Underfoot was one of those black and white cats that his father (who was a lawyer and very good with words) called "tuxedo cats." The lower part of his face was pure white, but the fur around his eyes was solid black in the shape of a mask. He sat rigidly still on his hind legs, with his white chest puffed out proudly between his black front legs, and he kept his pale gold eyes locked on Jimmy's brown ones.

At first, Jimmy thought Underfoot looked very brave and fierce. Then he saw how tiny and thin he

6

was. Underfoot was just a kitten. His pointy black ears and his pointy white whiskers were huge compared to the rest of him.

Jimmy couldn't help laughing out loud. When he did, Underfoot bolted away. Quick as a flash, Jimmy jumped up and yanked the window open, but the little cat was nowhere to be seen.

"Boy!" Jimmy muttered as he crawled back under the covers. "Underfoot may not be as mighty as he thinks he is, but he sure does come and go as he pleases!"

T W O
=== CRASH LANDING ===

Mandy and Doug O'Brien were Jimmy's new friends from apartment 4A. The next morning, they dropped by just as the Clarks were finishing breakfast. While Jimmy swallowed the last of his toast, he looked carefully at Mandy and Doug. He still found it hard to believe that they were twins. Mandy was tall and slim, and her hair was so blonde it was almost white. Doug was short, stocky, and redheaded. But they were both lots of fun, and since they were nine years old, like Jimmy—and the only other kids in the building— they had made friends with Jimmy right away.

"Hi, Mr. and Mrs. Clark," Mandy and Doug said cheerfully as they entered the kitchen. Then Doug turned to Jimmy and got straight to the point. "Want to come downstairs and try out my new robot? Dad brought it home yesterday from Chicago!"

"Extendo is not a robot, he's a remote control action figure," Mandy interrupted. "And he belongs to both of us!"

"Can I run Extendo by myself?" Jimmy asked.

Doug and Mandy looked at each other.

"Okay," said Doug at last.

"All right," Mandy agreed.

The three of them excused themselves from the kitchen and ran downstairs to the O'Briens' apartment.

Jimmy loved Mandy's and Doug's rec room. On one wall was an enormous mirror over a mat where Mandy practiced her gymnastics. The wall across the room was covered with Doug's posters of the planets and his giant star chart. He drew a red circle around each star he studied through his telescope. In between the two walls was a window overlooking Washington Street. A wooden bench decorated with decals stood in front of the window, and a yellow awning hung outside.

Jimmy, Doug, and Mandy sprawled on the floor,

and the twins introduced Jimmy to Extendo. Extendo was a foot-high plastic man who could walk and run, plus he could grasp, carry, drop, stack, or throw small objects at the press of a button.

"Do either of you guys know anything about Underfoot the cat?" Jimmy asked, as they took turns playing with Extendo.

"I do," shouted Mandy and Doug at the same time.

"Underfoot ripped into the garbage bag in our hallway one night," said Doug, holding his hand across his sister's mouth and letting Extendo crash into the mirror. "The next morning there were coffee grounds, chicken bones, and tin cans all over the place."

"And one day last week Underfoot got into a fight with Napoleon. Napoleon is Mr. Dupree's poodle," Mandy sputtered, jerking her brother's hand away from her mouth. "They were making a lot of noise and breaking stuff and Mom had to call the building superintendent."

Jimmy, Mandy, and Doug forgot about Extendo. The robot lay on his side, clutching a seashell and staring at his reflection in the mirror.

Meanwhile, Mandy and Doug told story after story about the things Underfoot had done, or the things people in the building *thought* Underfoot had done. They told more stories during a lunch of bologna and jelly sandwiches. And they were still talking about Underfoot after lunch, as they walked back to Jimmy's apartment to watch the workman put up wallpaper in the living room.

"I think Underfoot lives on the roof," Doug said, "but Mandy thinks—"

"There he is!" shrieked Mandy, before her brother could finish. "There's Underfoot!"

Sure enough, Jimmy caught sight of a black tail with a white tip disappearing through the open door of his very own apartment!

"Quick! Run!" Jimmy shouted, and they dashed to the end of the corridor. But there was no sign of Underfoot. In fact, no one was in the apartment except the workman, who was pasting a sheet of ivy-patterned wallpaper.

The three friends searched every corner of every room.

"Cats like to crawl into small places," said

Doug, so they looked under the couch and inside the rolled carpets.

"They also like machines that make steady noises," said Mandy, so they looked in back of the refrigerator and behind the grandfather clock.

Nowhere did they find Underfoot.

"I bet he squeezed through my bedroom window and out onto the fire escape," said Jimmy. "He sure is slippery!"

"I'll say!" Mandy agreed.

Doug and Mandy left then. Jimmy watched the workman put up the wallpaper, but he was really waiting for Underfoot to show up. As he looked around the living room, he noticed a small bulge in the sheet that covered the floor. He turned away. When he turned back, the bulge had moved. It was a whole foot closer to the stepladder the workman was standing on.

Jimmy crept toward the bulge and pounced on it. A small creature squirmed out of his grasp and sped toward the stepladder, pulling the sheet with it as it ran.

Ka-boom! The stepladder toppled.

"Yikes!" the workman shouted. He fell to the floor, tangled up in gooey wallpaper.

Jimmy stopped to help the workman and the bulge shot off toward the window, still dragging the sheet. The workman saw the moving bulge and yelled, "Grab that thing before—"

Ker-splash! The bucket of wallpaper paste flipped over, and thick, white liquid oozed across the living room floor.

At that moment, the creature burst out from under the sheet and leaped up to the window sill. But it leaped too hard. Jimmy froze as he watched Underfoot sail past the sill, through the window and into open space!

"Underfoot! Oh, no! Underfoot!" Jimmy cried.

"What on earth is Underfoot?" the workman muttered. He scrambled around, trying to mop up the wallpaper paste with old newspapers.

"He's a cat, that's what!" Jimmy wailed. He ran to the window and looked down.

There was Underfoot, below him, smack in the middle of the yellow awning outside of Mandy's and Doug's rec room. Several of the snaps holding

the awning to its frame had popped open, and the cloth strained against the others.

Underfoot was clinging to the cloth with his sharp claws, but his four little legs were shaking. He stared up at Jimmy, opened his mouth, and made a frantic meow for help.

"I'm coming, Underfoot!" Jimmy called. "Hold on!"

Jimmy tore past the grumbling workman, out his front door, and down the corridor to the stairway. It took him only seconds to reach the front door to apartment 4A. He pounded furiously on it. "Mandy! Doug!" he shouted. "Let me in, quick!"

Mrs. O'Brien threw open the door. "Jimmy!" she exclaimed. "What's wrong? Mandy and Doug went outside—"

"Sorry, Mrs. O'Brien. Underfoot's caught in your awning," Jimmy said, panting as he fled past her to the playroom. He jumped onto the wooden bench below the window sill and pulled down the top window. Half of the awning flapped loose in the wind. Underfoot was clinging to the other half—but just barely.

"Don't budge," Jimmy said softly. "Keep cool,

Underfoot." Jimmy tenderly lifted him off the awning, drew him inside, and cradled him in his arms. Underfoot didn't move a muscle.

"Jimmy, how's Underfoot?" Mrs. O'Brien asked. She had followed them into the rec room. One look at them, and she knew she should stay very calm and quiet.

"Why don't you take Underfoot upstairs?" she whispered. "I'll find Mandy and Doug and tell them what's happened."

"Thanks a lot, Mrs. O'Brien," Jimmy answered. Carefully he carried Underfoot out to the hallway and back upstairs to his apartment. Underfoot never took his eyes off Jimmy.

THREE
==== NOISES IN THE NIGHT ====

"**H**ere's Underfoot," Jimmy whispered to the workman, who was leaving the Clarks' apartment with an armload of wet newspapers when Jimmy reached the front door.

"Hmmph!" replied the workman, with an angry glance. Large scraps of wallpaper were stuck to his overalls. He looked as if he had just hacked his way through an ivy patch.

When Jimmy reached the kitchen, he placed Underfoot on the floor and looked at him sternly. "Stay put this time, Underfoot," Jimmy warned.

Underfoot sat like a statue as Jimmy got a carton of milk and a saucer, and poured some milk out for Underfoot.

"This is for you, Underfoot," Jimmy said, setting the saucer on the floor. "Come have a drink."

Jimmy waited, but Underfoot wouldn't stir. He just stared at Jimmy, his giant whiskers bristling out from either side of his tiny nose. He looked like a little troublemaker who had been forced to stay in a corner and didn't feel a bit guilty.

Jimmy had an idea. He went back to the refrigerator, opened it, and pretended to look for something inside. Through the crack in the door, he saw Underfoot step over to the saucer and begin to lap up the milk.

A knock sounded at the front door then. Jimmy closed the refrigerator gently, and tiptoed past Underfoot to answer it.

"Where is he?" shouted Mandy and Doug, barging into the hall as soon as Jimmy opened the door.

"Shh!" Jimmy waved his hands back and forth to silence them. "Follow me." He led them quietly into the kitchen. There was the saucer—half full—but Underfoot was nowhere to be seen.

"I can't believe it!" Jimmy cried. "Underfoot's gone *again!*"

"Don't panic," Doug said. "Let's check every-where. He's got to be nearby."

Doug, Mandy, and Jimmy set out to search the apartment for the second time that day. They began with the living room, even though the living room door was tightly closed.

"No, that little varmint is definitely *not* here," the workman exclaimed from the top of his ladder. "Believe me, I made sure of it! Now shut that door!"

Underfoot wasn't in any of the other rooms either, at least as far as Mandy, Doug, and Jimmy could tell.

"Your bedroom window is still open," Doug pointed out. "He must be getting in and out through there."

Jimmy groaned, stormed over to the window, and slammed it shut. Then the three of them slumped into chairs around the kitchen table.

"You know, guys, after today I could draw a picture of every square inch of this apartment with my eyes shut!" Mandy moaned.

"Yeah, and that's probably how you searched it," Doug teased her.

Mandy was too worn out to start an argument. "Come on, let's go home, Doug," she said with a sigh. "One thing you can say about Extendo—he doesn't run out on you!"

"Bye, Jimmy," Doug said. "And good-bye, Underfoot, if you can hear me."

That evening, Jimmy was so sad that his mother and father didn't scold him about the mess Underfoot had made in the living room.

"I'm sure Underfoot is very grateful to you, Jimmy. You saved his life," his mother said. She handed him a bunch of photographs. "Why don't you look at those and try to forget about Underfoot while your father and I make dinner?"

Jimmy looked at his mother's prints of the Mickey Mouse squash, the corkscrew carrot, and the high-heeled banana, but even they couldn't make him laugh.

After a silent dinner, Jimmy's father said, "Son, it's not like you to be so upset. Is Underfoot all that's bothering you, or is there something else?"

Jimmy saw how worried his father was. "Well," he said at last, "I've been pretty bored since we moved here, Dad. The only friends I have are Doug and Mandy, and they spend a lot of time by themselves. I was hoping maybe I could keep Underfoot as a pet."

"I see," Mr. Clark replied. The worried look was gone from his face, but Jimmy couldn't tell what his father was thinking now. "How do you feel about that, Beth?" he asked Mrs. Clark.

"I like the idea," she answered. "Having a cat around would liven this place up."

"That's just it, Dad," Jimmy agreed. "Underfoot would be a lot of fun. I'm sure he'd settle down and be a good cat if he had a real home."

His father frowned thoughtfully. "It is difficult getting used to a new place," he said slowly. "And I know you're a responsible person. I don't object to your keeping Underfoot, *if* you take him to the veterinarian right away for a check-up, and *if* you take care of him and keep him under control."

"I promise!" Jimmy cried.

"Now why don't we hunt through the apartment one more time," his mother suggested with a smile. "Maybe Underfoot is still in hiding somewhere."

Jimmy and his parents searched and they searched, but they could not find Underfoot.

"He's bound to turn up sooner or later," Mr. Clark said as he spooned up three dishes of Jimmy's favorite ice cream—peanut brittle and vanilla.

"Yeah, I'm sure he will," Jimmy answered, but he wasn't sure at all. He was just being polite. "Where could Underfoot *possibly* be?" he wondered. And then a horrible thought came to him. "He could be across the city by now, that's where! Someone else might have him!"

That night Jimmy propped his bedroom window open with a ruler. Then he crawled into bed and lay there, gazing out at the full moon.

"Underfoot, Underfoot," he called softly into the night.

Jimmy waited and waited, but Underfoot didn't come. At last Jimmy gave up and rolled over, reaching his arm around his pillow as he always did when he was ready to go to sleep.

This time the pillow made a strange, raggedy noise, a sort of buzz and hum. Jimmy lifted it up and there lay Underfoot, purring away. The kitten

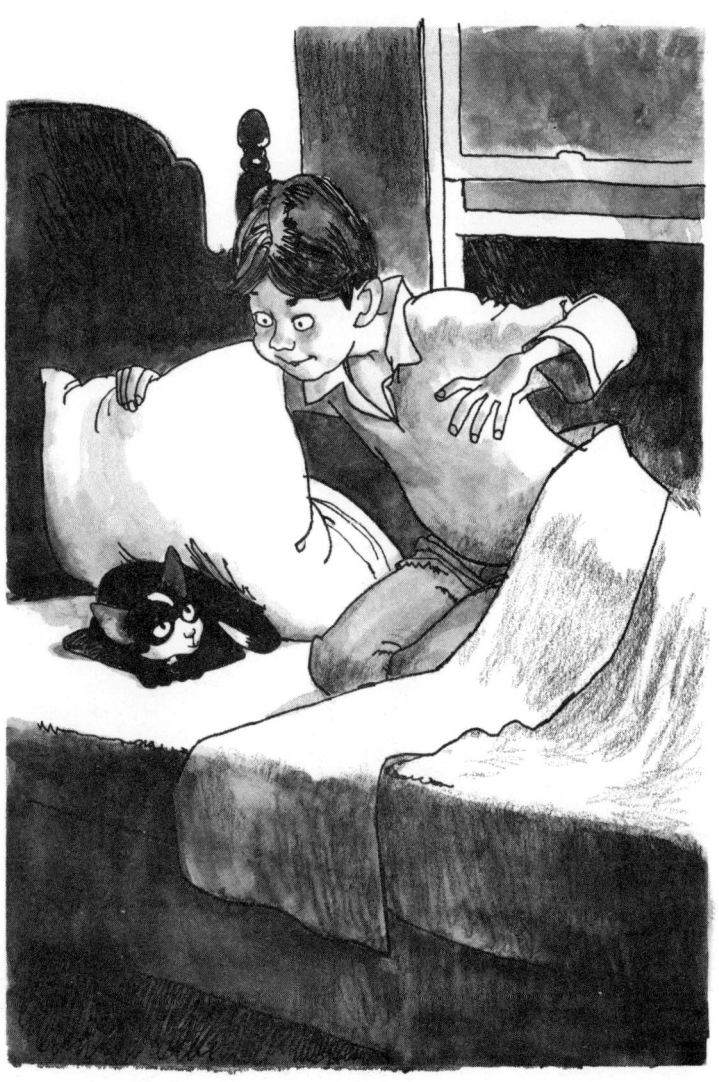

opened his big gold eyes and stared at Jimmy. Then he crawled across the bed and nestled against Jimmy's side.

Jimmy didn't move a muscle, except for the ones around his mouth, which broke into a big smile. "Tomorrow I'll take Underfoot to the vet and tell him he's *my* cat. Then he'll be registered in my name," he told himself. And he thought about his new pet until both he and Underfoot fell asleep.

MORE TROUBLE

O N E

$=$ A SURPRISE BIRTHDAY GUEST $=$

Jimmy Clark was dreaming about tigers. Six of them were pacing around a large cage. Jimmy was standing in the middle. He cracked his whip once and the tigers stopped in their tracks. He cracked his whip twice and the tigers stood up on their hind legs. He cracked his whip three times and—

"Hey! Watch out!"

Jimmy's eyes popped open. It was his father's voice, coming from the kitchen. Then he heard a heavy, dull thud and felt the wall shake. He jumped out of bed and pulled on his jeans.

"Are you okay, dear?" This time it was his mother's voice, coming from his parents' bedroom at the other end of the apartment.

"Yes, Beth. I'm all right," his father shouted back. "You stay there!"

Jimmy ran into the kitchen. His father was sprawled on the kitchen floor with his hands spread flat beside each shoulder, and his elbows stuck straight up into the air. In his green bathrobe he looked like an enormous grasshopper.

"Dad, what are you doing?" Jimmy asked.

"What do you think I'm doing? Push-ups?" his father grumbled. He struggled to his knees. "Something—Underfoot, I assume—darted out of nowhere, ran right under my feet, and tripped me."

Mr. Clark was back on his feet. "Look at this mess!" he exclaimed. The front of his bathrobe was smeared with yellowish goo. And on the floor below him was a smashed gray cardboard carton. It was soaking wet and dotted all over with pieces of eggshell.

"Gosh, Dad, I'm sorry!" Jimmy said. "Where did Underfoot go? Did he get hurt?"

Mr. Clark glared at Jimmy for a moment. Then his face softened. "I'm sure Underfoot is fine," he

said. "He ran behind the refrigerator and if he's smart, he'll stay there for a while."

Jimmy peered into the narrow space between the back of the refrigerator and the wall. Sure enough, beaming at him like two tiny flashlights was a pair of gold eyes. Underfoot—the mysterious kitten who had been prowling Jimmy's building for weeks—was still inside his very own apartment!

"Leave him alone for now, Jimmy," Mr. Clark said. "Come help me clean up."

Jimmy pulled some paper towels from the roller above the sink. He began wiping the broken eggs from the floor. "Underfoot was hiding in my bed when I went to sleep last night," Jimmy explained. "He really likes it here, Dad. And you said if I took care of him I could keep him—"

"And you *may* keep him," interrupted his father, who was dabbing his egg-smeared bathrobe with a damp washcloth. "We'll just have to get used to him. He won't always be so little and so frisky and so sneaky. I hope."

"Wow! Thanks, Dad!" Jimmy cried with relief.

"Right now, I have a job for you," Mr. Clark said. "Your mother has been working very hard on her photographs lately, so I'm fixing her breakfast in bed for her birthday. Would you please wrap her presents while I cook the two eggs that are left. There's ribbon and paper on the table."

"Sure, Dad," Jimmy replied.

"Then, after breakfast, you can go shopping," his father continued. "We need more eggs, and Underfoot needs cat food, kitty litter, and a litter box. I'll give you some money and you can go across the street to Shaheen's Grocery Store, okay?"

"You bet!" Jimmy agreed.

Jimmy carefully wrapped his mother's birthday presents. He and his father had bought her a bottle of gardenia perfume, a book about Eskimos, and a wide-brimmed straw hat in an old-fashioned hatbox. Every few seconds Jimmy would glance back at the refrigerator, but Underfoot seemed happy to stay hidden. While Jimmy worked, his father prepared a breakfast of eggs sunny-side-up, toast, and orange juice.

"Happy birthday!" Jimmy and his father cried. They strode through the bedroom doorway with the gifts and the breakfast tray for Jimmy's mother.

"Now this is how I like to start the day!" exclaimed Mrs. Clark. She sat up in the bed, grinning.

When Jimmy's mother had finished her breakfast and admired her presents, Jimmy told her how he had found Underfoot in his bed, and how Underfoot had slept all night with him. Neither Jimmy nor his father mentioned the broken eggs.

"I'm glad Underfoot has adopted us," his mother joked. "But remember, Jimmy, you have to take him to the vet first thing. Can you manage it by yourself?"

"Sure," Jimmy answered. "I'll take him to Dr. van Taller, I guess. He's right down the block. As soon as Underfoot's ready, we'll go. He's resting behind the refrigerator right now."

No sooner were these words out of Jimmy's mouth, than a blurry bundle of fur shot through the doorway and jumped onto the bed. Several long strands of bright red ribbon were dangling from its mouth.

"Guard the tray!" Jimmy shrieked. "It's Underfoot!"

Jimmy's mother grabbed her orange juice in one

hand and her coffee in the other. Jimmy's father yanked the tray from her lap. Underfoot galloped across the mattress, shedding ribbon in his path. Then he leaped off the other side of the bed and dived underneath it.

Mrs. Clark scrambled to her feet, spilling the covers and her presents over the side of the bed, just as Underfoot ran out. For a few seconds, Underfoot was trapped beneath the covers. Then the strong smell of gardenias filled the air. The covers shook frantically and Jimmy heard a loud *hiss*. Underfoot broke loose and bolted out of the room. This time he was trailing the scent of gardenias.

Jimmy and his parents glanced sideways at each other. Then they burst out laughing. "That was a very exciting way to end the party!" Jimmy's mother said, stooping to pick up her presents.

"And I don't think you'll have any problem tracking Underfoot now, Jimmy," his father added. "Just follow your nose!"

T W O

══ STARTING OFF WITH A BANG ══

Jimmy burst through the swinging screen door of Shaheen's Grocery Store.

"Whoa, Jimmy!" called Mr. Shaheen, waving his hands. He stood behind the counter and looked alarmed. But then he always looked alarmed. His thick glasses made his eyes appear twice as big as they actually were. "What's the hurry?" he asked.

"I've got a cat, Mr. Shaheen," Jimmy announced proudly. "His name is Underfoot. I need cat food, kitty litter, a litter box, and a dozen eggs."

"A dozen eggs?" Mr. Shaheen repeated. "I guess you plan to feed Underfoot well!"

"Oh, no," replied Jimmy. "The eggs are for my parents and me. I'm not sure what cats eat."

"Well, you have quite a choice," Mr. Shaheen told Jimmy, as he walked to the back of the store.

Shaheen's Grocery Store was small, but it was crammed with all kinds of food, cleaning supplies, and other interesting things. Sometimes Jimmy went to Shaheen's just to look around and see what was what.

Jimmy followed Mr. Shaheen to the pet food shelf. He groaned when he saw the stacks and stacks of cat food. There were orange boxes, green boxes, brown boxes, candy-striped boxes and even checkerboard boxes. And there were cans—some big, some small, in all different colors, with pictures of cats and kittens on them.

"Which ones should I take, Mr. Shaheen?" Jimmy asked, frowning.

"That depends," said Mr. Shaheen. "How old is Underfoot?"

"I'm not sure," Jimmy answered. "But he's very smart and independent. He's been feeding himself for several weeks now."

"Is he a big cat?" Mr. Shaheen asked.

"Not *very* big," Jimmy admitted. He held out his hands, a little less than a foot apart.

"Ah, a compact model." Mr. Shaheen said, reaching toward the shelf containing food especially for kittens. "Then you should take some of this dry food in the purple box, and some of this wet food in the can with the alley cat on the label."

Jimmy took several boxes and cans, and Mr. Shaheen gathered the rest of the items: a bag of Desert Dry Kitty Litter, a blue plastic litter box, and a box of jumbo-size eggs.

When Jimmy returned to the apartment, he set the littler box in the bathroom. Then he put a bowl of cat food (half dry, half wet) on the kitchen floor. He sniffed the air for gardenias and followed the flowery smell past his mother, who was reading her Eskimo book at the kitchen table, and over to the back of the stove, where the smell was particularly strong.

"Underfoot, Underfoot," he called softly into the dark space. But Underfoot wouldn't budge. His shining eyes told intruders not to bother him.

"Give Underfoot time," his mother advised. "He has to decide for himself that he wants to come out and behave."

Jimmy plopped down in a chair across from his mother and kept his eyes on the stove. The apartment became so quiet that he could hear birds chirping outside and the hum of traffic on Washington Street.

Jimmy had just decided that he couldn't wait any longer, when a twitching pink nose emerged from behind the stove, followed by long white whiskers, two eyes surrounded by a black fur mask, two huge ears, a small black and white body, and, finally, a slender black tail with a white tip. Looking neither right nor left, Underfoot slinked over to the bowl Jimmy had placed on the floor. He began nibbling his food.

"Why, Underfoot is adorable!" exclaimed Jimmy's mother, who was seeing him closely for the first time. "And he's so tiny!"

"He's bigger than he looks, Mom," Jimmy replied. "And he can be pretty fierce when he needs to be."

"Let's hope he doesn't get fierce too often," she said. "Anyway, now that Underfoot is out, you can take him to the vet. I have a box that will be perfect for carrying him."

Mrs. Clark left the kitchen. When she returned, she was carrying the box that had held her straw hat. It was pink with small bunches of daisies printed all over it.

"Aw, Mom!" Jimmy cried. "I can't carry Underfoot in *that* box!"

"I'm afraid it's the only box here that's strong enough," his mother told him. "It's a good size, too. You can get a carrying case before he has to go to the vet again. Here, let's poke a few holes in the hatbox so Underfoot can breathe. Then tie the lid down with a piece of rope and you're in business."

Jimmy was worried that Underfoot might vanish again unless he acted fast, so he did what his mother suggested. By the time Underfoot had finished eating, the box was ready.

Jimmy knealed down, placed the box on the floor, and called, "Underfoot! Underfoot!" To Jimmy's surprise, Underfoot trotted over to the box and began sniffing it. And then he jumped inside! Instantly, Jimmy clapped the lid on top of the box and tied the rope around it.

"Bye, Mom!" said Jimmy, and off he went to Dr. van Taller's, the box jiggling as Underfoot batted his paws against it. Every now and then Underfoot meowed, or thrust his pink nose out of a breathing hole, and Jimmy felt sorry that he had to confine him. Underfoot wasn't used to being cooped up. The two-block walk to the vet's seemed endless, but at last they reached the office.

Jimmy slowly opened the door to Dr. van Taller's animal clinic and peered inside. All the seats in the room were full. On the chair nearest the door sat a short woman holding a leash with a big Irish setter on the other end. Next to her sat a bald man balancing a cage with a parrot in it on his lap. Next to him sat a freckle-faced girl. On the floor at her feet rested a curious black case with a screened window. And on a couch directly across the room sat a gray-haired woman and a gray-haired man stroking a fat, mean-looking tabby cat.

Dr. van Taller's assistant, Ms. Nelson, was perched behind a desk facing the doorway. Jimmy stepped over to her. "This is my new kitten, Underfoot," Jimmy announced. He placed the hatbox containing Underfoot on Ms. Nelson's desk. "He needs a check-up and his shots."

Ms. Nelson untied the knot and peeked inside

the box. "Oh, isn't he cute!" she exclaimed. "And what a cute little carrying box! It smells like gardenias!"

Jimmy's face turned red and he swallowed hard.

"And what is your name, young man?" Ms. Nelson asked.

"Jimmy Clark," he answered, "We live at 237 Washington Street." Ms. Nelson wrote the information down on a pale blue card.

"And what is your phone number?" she asked.

Ka-pow! Outside, a car suddenly backfired.

Quick as a flash, Underfoot sprang out of the hatbox and ran into the waiting room. The mean-looking tabby cat broke away from his owners and charged after him. They raced past the Irish setter, who lunged away from *her* owner and chased after *them*, barking furiously. Then the setter's leash snagged the bald man's foot and pulled it sharply out from under him.

Ka-boing! The cage fell from the bald man's lap and started bouncing across the floor. The cage door sprang open. The parrot flew out, squawking, and circled above the other animals, who ran around and around the waiting room.

43

Thud! The bouncing cage finally landed on the case at the freckle-faced girl's feet, knocking it open. Out slid a long, fat, green and brown snake. The snake slithered under the chairs toward the couch.

"Ew! Eek!" All the people in the room— except for the freckle-faced girl—squealed and jumped up onto their seats.

Underfoot, the tabby cat, the Irish setter, the parrot, and the snake were still mewing and barking and squawking and slithering, when the door suddenly swung open and Officer Roseberg, the neighborhood patrolwoman, stepped inside.

"What's going on in here?" Officer Roseberg cried. She shut the door behind her quickly—but just before it closed, Underfoot darted outside.

"Underfoot! Oh, no! Underfoot!" Jimmy yelped. He hurtled over the animals, past Officer Roseberg, and out into the street.

Jimmy looked all around, but Underfoot was nowhere in sight! Where had he gone?

THREE
═ What Goes Up Must Come ═ Down

Jimmy ran down Washington Street toward his apartment building. He stopped everyone he met and asked, "Did you see a black and white cat go by?" But each person replied, "No, I'm sorry." One man said he had noticed a cocker spaniel on the other side of the street, and a woman who was jogging said she had passed a large brown cat, but no one had seen Underfoot.

"I've blown it!" Jimmy thought miserably. "This was my first time out with Underfoot, and I lost him. He must be hiding again."

Jimmy explored every possible hiding place he could see. He peeked into some big pipes lying in front of the hardware store. He searched under the cars parked along the sidewalk. He poked his head into some empty crates piled next to a trash bin. Everywhere he went he sniffed the air, hoping to catch the scent of gardenias. But all he smelled was the city—asphalt, exhaust, and trash.

Underfoot, the master escape artist, had done it again!

After a long time, Jimmy found himself standing in front of Shaheen's Grocery Store. He stepped inside. "Hi, Mr. Shaheen," he said. "Remember Underfoot, the cat I told you about? He's missing! He's black and white and looks like he's wearing a robber's mask. Have you seen him?"

"I'm sorry, Jimmy. I haven't," Mr. Shaheen answered, shaking his head sadly.

"Underfoot? Gone?" Doug O'Brien's voice came from the next aisle. Jimmy headed toward it, and the two friends bumped into each other at the front of the store.

"What happened?" Doug asked.

Jimmy told him the whole story, from finding Underfoot in his bed the night before, to what happened in Dr. van Taller's clinic.

Doug lowered his head and thought for a moment. "I've got it," he said at last. "Why don't we go back to the clinic and ask Officer Roseberg to help us look for Underfoot? She's probably used to this sort of thing."

"That's a good idea," Jimmy said, feeling a little better. He smiled at Doug, and the two of them dashed down Washington Street.

When Jimmy opened the door to Dr. van Taller's clinic, the waiting room looked quite different from the way it had when he'd left it. The short woman and her Irish setter were gone. The bald man stood in a corner clutching his caged parrot tightly to his chest. The freckle-faced girl was kneeling on the floor, winding a thick black cord around the snake's case. The gray-haired woman was waving a newspaper over the gray-haired man, who lay stretched out on the couch. And Ms. Nelson was pinning the mean-looking tabby to her desk with both hands. Officer Roseberg stood beside her, writing in a little notebook.

"Officer Roseberg!" Jimmy cried. "I've lost Underfoot, my cat. He's gone. What should I do?"

"He's fast on his feet and very good at disappearing," Doug added.

"Is Underfoot the little black and white tornado that was here awhile ago?" Officer Roseberg asked.

"That's the one!" Ms. Nelson snapped.

"Well, chances are he didn't go too far," Officer Roseberg said. "Where have you looked?"

"I went up and down Washington Street," Jimmy replied. "I asked people whether they'd seen him and they all said they hadn't. Then I looked inside pipes and boxes and under cars and he wasn't anywhere."

"Hmmm," Officer Roseberg murmured. "Nobody saw him? Did you look up? Into the trees?"

"Into the trees?" Jimmy repeated. "No. Do you think Underfoot really climbed up a tree?"

"Lots of cats do that when they're scared," Doug said. "Come on. Let's check!"

Jimmy and Doug ran outside. They stopped at the first tree they reached, gazing up into the leaves and branches. They were looking for a sign of black and white fur, but all they saw was a beat-up kite and a robin's nest.

They moved on to the next tree—an especially tall maple at the corner of the block. The leaves were dense and it was hard to see much, but suddenly Jimmy shouted, "I smell gardenias!" He heard a rustling noise far above. A breeze blew some leaves aside, and there was Underfoot! He was perched at the very top of the tree, clinging to a branch that seemed too small to hold him.

"Hang on, Underfoot!" Jimmy called to him. He jumped up and grabbed a branch above his head. Then he swung himself toward the trunk of the tree to get a good foothold.

"Be careful, Jimmy!" Doug shouted. "Take it easy. Underfoot's not going anywhere."

Jimmy slowly made his way up the tree. He tested each branch before he put his weight on it. The top of the tree looked much farther away than it had from the ground, and the thick mass of leaves and branches kept him from seeing Underfoot. Finally, he felt that he couldn't climb any higher. He stopped at a big fork in the trunk of the tree to get his bearings.

"How's it going?" Doug called from below.

Jimmy looked down at the street and caught his

breath in surprise. There stood not only Doug, but Officer Roseberg, Ms. Nelson, the bald man with the parrot, the freckle-faced girl with the snake, the gray-haired couple (without the tabby cat), and even Mr. Shaheen—all with their eyes on Jimmy.

"I'm fine!" Jimmy shouted down, feeling very brave. "But I can't see Underfoot!"

"He's right over your head!" Doug yelled back.

Jimmy peered into the leaves above him. "Underfoot, Underfoot," he called.

Suddenly the branch above him banged into his head. Jimmy felt little claws digging into his left shoulder. Underfoot! He braced himself more securely against the trunk and pulled Underfoot into his arms.

"I've got him!" he cried to the people below.

"All *right!*" Doug shouted, and the crowd burst into applause.

Jimmy looked down at Underfoot. "You're some climber!" he said. Underfoot just stared back at him, his eyes shining mysteriously from their black fur mask. Then he relaxed in Jimmy's arms and started purring.

That night at dinner, Jimmy proudly showed his

parents the certificate that Dr. van Taller had given him after Underfoot had finally had his check-up. It listed "Jimmy Clark" as Underfoot's owner!

Then Jimmy told them the story of Underfoot's adventure. He pointed out how fearless Underfoot had been, not only while he was caught in the top of the tree, but also while he was getting his shots. Underfoot didn't even fidget when Dr. van Taller gave him a bath!

"And where is the courageous Underfoot now?" Mr. Clark asked.

"Oh, he's resting behind the stove again," Jimmy answered casually. "I think he's cooking up his next life!"

Read about Underfoot's next lives
in *The Many Lives of Underfoot the Cat:*
HIT THE ROAD and STRIKE IT RICH
(available May 1991)

About the Author and Illustrator

JACK MAGUIRE graduated from Columbia College and received a Masters in Literature from Boston University. He has taught literature at Memphis State University and has worked with the learning disabled. He currently is a freelance writer and conducts storytelling workshops and programs in the New York City school system. Camping and hiking are among his hobbies, and he has travelled through Europe, the Soviet Union, and the Caribbean. Underfoot is based on his own black and white cat, Overton. He lives in Highland, New York.

SANDY KOSSIN is originally from Los Angeles but he has lived in New York for most of his life. He has been painting for thirty-five years and has received numerous awards from the Society of Illustrators. He is married and lives in Port Washington, New York.

POCKET BOOKS PRESENTS

MINSTREL BOOKS™

THE FUN BOOKS YOU WILL NOT WANT TO MISS!!